after
thought

Carl Watson

Other books by Carl Watson

Stage Fright (Apathy Press)
Only Descend (Autonomedia)
Pareidolia (Autonomendia)
Idylls of Complicity (Spuyten Duyvil)
Astral Botanica (Fly By Night)
Backwards the Drowned Go Dreaming (Sensitive Skin)
Psychosomatic Life (vagabonde)
Belle Catastrophe (Colophon)
The Hotel of Irrevocable Acts (Autonomedia)
Beneath the Empire of the Birds (Apathy)
Bricolage ex Machina (Lost Modern)
Anarcadium Pan (Erie Street)

ISBN: 9798841818984

Some of these poems in one form or another have appeared in:
evergreen gazette, ritual sex, psychosomatic life, and elsewhere.

Special thanks to Tom DiVenti and Dick Turner
Cover design by Chris Brunt
Cover art by Charles Schick

Apathy Press Books are published and distributed by

Apathy Press
Baltimore, NYC, Paris, Cosmos

Together with the previous volume, *Stage Fright*, this book completes a set of what might be called new and selected poems. The various pieces in these two volumes were written over a period of several decades, from the late 1970s to the present. The variety of "styles" is due both to the time period and location: Portland, New Orleans, Chicago, New York, Fleischmanns and Paris.

The quotes at the beginning of each chapter are all translations of the writings of Matsuo Basho and they have little relation to the poems that follow them.

contents

dream life of a weather beaten skeleton

excavations of intimacy

barrel-fire songs and back-alley ballads

random scenes from silent film scripts

after thoughts of a travel-worn satchel

after thought

dreamlife of a weather-beaten skeleton

"I set out on a journey of a thousand leagues, packing no provisions. I leaned on the staff of an ancient who, it is said, entered into nothingness under the midnight moon."

gentrification

The poet is always in search
Of "the Way" in a wayfaring life.
The metaphor of mental "home"
Being never secure. A broke-down box truck,
Or an old fishing/hunting hut could do.
Viaducts, unused tunnels too,
Or empty shipping containers
In back alleys, back lots, backyards
Or sheltered corners on backstreets,

Approached in a spirit of domesticity
Each can be renovated to suit:
Curtains hung in the windows
Of an abandoned car make a living room,
A hot water bottle and a large salad bowl
Work well for a kitchen sink.
A desk of pallet board planks in a rusted
School bus create office space
For the gig worker of visionary verse.

The open outhouse of forest and meadow
Requires no plumbing or disinfectant
And lets the privates breathe.
An hour's walk to a shop for bread
Whisky and canned goods is no problem
When one wears the old long-coat
Burden of nomadic words.
The heavy boots of human sorrow
Bring ballast to the wandering step.

Satchel and staff serve the alienated
Pilgrim on surrounding roads.
He knows soon enough the crowds
Will come to celebrate his sacrifice.
Real estate speculation will rise
And one more scribe will be forced
To move on to a further edge
Of the hungry consuming world,
Seeking new visions to market.

cipher

He stands before all, unjudged,
A life without ads or advocate
This is the Way of the vagabond poet,
No real purpose or significance to it
He may solicit condemnation,
If that's all you have to give,
At least you give that much.
His rhymes may not impress
In contrast to those spectacles
Generated by the beast
Of a billion starburst terminals,
Yet he carries his ragged banner
Down the high-wired street, anyway,
Often unseen by neighbors,
Police, or the humanitarian, empathetic
Drone minds of arts and letters.
But it's alright, it's ok, no problem,
He no longer needs to cry out
"Notice me!" or "Be my friend!"
Within the market din, the demanding stare
Which asks the same tax of everyone,
Only louder and faster each day,
And all the time and everywhere.

mimic

He is often a mimic with no set identity,
What many distrust and shun.
They can't draw a bead on or fix
For certain, his style or reason to exist.
He's traveled to many cities,
Too many, and never found a fit.
The roads to and from can't
Properly monetize his steps.
No chic, no genre, no clichéd essence,
Nor can any glass flatter
His backward looking fashion,
But it's alright, it's ok. He doesn't mind
Because words aren't scaffolds anymore
To shore up his broke down heart.
Instead, they release the pressure
Of one that's overfull, expressed
Like the cuttlefish who blows
An ink-black screen by which to flee
Enemies in a hostile ocean—
This poet's words make a similar confusion
To hide behind, and at the same time
Diffuse himself—to enter nothingness
In the effort to merge with a world
That's always too much and too little,
Too near and too far.

And when he enters the gates of Anytown
With his sandwiches and coffee,
He will bear no presence, no history,
No baggage, no past exploits
Or generations—nothing but everything
Comes with him to entertain the masses.
A man of the moment, not
More or less, and when he leaves,
Within seconds, memory dies,
Citizens forget his name and shape,
Though something in their lives has changed
And they might be grateful for that.

strayed muse

When the muse first arrived,
As a residue of long departed light,
A time exposed spirit trail
Of the long limbo-like ribbon
Of astral highway that bore her
Here, home through a magic night
It was ok, alright, and yet
He suspected there were no
Glory-bound roads as such,
And this animal, egg or automaton
Approaching with probable agenda
Was just one more pose of potential
Verging on commercial.
Therefore, as was the poet's habit,
He dressed the visitation with a face
From a harem of possibilities
Then started to write the verse
That tracked her journey to this place:
Timbuktu to Andromeda,
Titan Five to Present Time,
And the inspiration he chased
Through this self-made instigation—
Be it romantic ship, box car, book
Or barroom—it kept receding,
But he went on writing anyway,
As a path through the coming years
That would end somewhere:
At the edge of the marvelous,
At the spectacle of the grave,
At the ocean of the womb,
On the shore below the shuddering stars,
The end of all appetite and error
Beginning the gift of compassion.

little shop of carnivores

The stop was a congregation of urban clichés
Cops, pushers, addicts, preachers, the old school
Cat & mouse parade of poverty & segregation,
And always, the one sad bookseller living in his van.

Pushing his way through the crazy gauntlet,
Past unfinished dinners in Styrofoam trays,
Heroes, orange peels, abandoned on the sidewalk,
While radical screeds bloom on tenement walls,

He was taken back to his twenties, a green kid
In the city with a suitcase and a box lunch
Looking for work and thrills. No memory of
Where he was going, but it started while waiting

Underground for the D Train at West 4th:
A tout's business card slipped in his hand
For an occult bookshop in the 100s.
The slogan asked: "Ignorance is bliss?"

He remembers heading uptown straight off,
No plans anyway, no real mission,
But wanting to challenge the assumption
That he was immune to the charms of a stranger.

He knocked at the basement entrance,
It opened on its own. He rang the counter bell,
But no one came, so he pushed in further
To a backroom orgy of limbs, lips and ass.

He saw no whole faces, only mouths gaping
In Rituals of Spiritual Hunger, Sabbaths of Greed,
Bodies consuming their parts, ideas eating their own
Minds in a cult of Self Destruction.

A dancing Ringmaster Mouse strayed from
Youthful acid flashbacks employed a barbed lasso
Of light to form the double yoke of infinity,
Where the curious fell, seeking Alternative Life.

port of poor decisions

Once while shipping
On the Mere Incognito
He anchored in the harbor
Of The Port of Poor Decisions
A region of too well-known
Climate & tongue
On the southern shores
Of the Great Dead Lake.

The rough sawn café tables,
Were waited on by refugees
From other mill towns,
From wars of acquisition,
From despot states.
A chalkboard displayed
The day's blue-plate specials.

The staff wore their blouses
Strategically torn to exhibit
Bite scars born with cold pride
As abused youth will,
Just to make customers aware
Of their own early servitude
To unwanted trauma, emergencies

Of libido and overblown fortune,
That by which young women
In lamb-stained aprons
Steered the sad johns
To the split hip and garden hollow
Made available to every
Deprived mate for a price.

Conversations were held
Among fellow braggarts and hunters
Of those bold but cowardly days,
Men who didn't care much
For life or appearance,
As noted by their cracked teeth,
And scissor-cut mullets.

Tales were told of great disruptions,
Escapes from tunnels, prisons,
And what they termed
"The Return". For all return,
They smugly claimed,
Pointing to a staircase
At the far end of the room.

We all return! They sang, slamming
Their mugs in rhythm to the march
Of hardy souls, so many,
Answering their calling,
Brown ale bottles knocking
To the morbid chant,
Their tools at the ready.

Outside, troubadours sang
On street corners in tribute,
The café lights never dimmed
On that obscure street, that's true,
And many an old friend
Was never seen in the halo
Of his professed virtue again.

early light

The soft recitation of a single
Bland gray dove is heard
Over rush hour racket,
Long in plaint and invocation
Yet somehow soothing,
Perched on the stone sill
Of a filthy city window,
Gathering fresh daylight
As the poet rolls in musty quilts,
A limbo-loving hobo saint
Of half-sleep holding on
For one final foray, one
Last dance in prelude
To the false virgin of the new day,
He clogs and stomps,
Chicken walks and waltzes,
Steals with grasping hands
Along the jazz-jagged iron
Fire escapes that span his street,
Riding the thin red melody line,
Of horizon's glowing wire,
Then drops to the tar
Papered flat roofs, dotted
With mirrors of puddled rain
And dying lamp light,
Across spotted black casements
Where hatchling beaks beg
Regurgitated breakfast,
He walks narrow tightropes
Of washday gossip, union suits,
Bath towels, tennis shoes,
Dangled by their laces
Over market barkers' bad jokes,
Fish scale stardust, sausage smoke,
Cilantro, anchos, juju roots,
Sporting a crushed felt hat, a broken tooth,
Like some Dickensian orphan
Or Krishna on a butter quest,
With a handful of the sweet yellow
Folded like dream embryos
In a day-old crust,

He smells hot coffee vicariously
In the kitchens of shift workers,
He wanders the girders,
An unnoticed voyeur, outcast
From everyday community,
Searching the odd and unknown
Scales of pedestrian song,
And his feet are the prongs of a player
On the steel steps of keyboards,
And the city is a sheaf of scores,
At one with many instruments
For tongues and anxious fingers,
Where the poet throws orchestral eyes,
Reader of mystic keys and speeds,
With pockets full of word spore,
Root balls, thunder clouds,
Alien seeds and cryptic codes
To countless untold doors.

insomnia

The poet gets ideas for lines
And fancy phrases in the borderland
Between sleep and waking,
That dreamscape of miracle and chaos
Long wandered as avatar,
And holograph, a hobo ghost,
And he has to decide,
Should he turn on the light
To write the great vision down,
The uncanny musical passage,
Played by rogue harlequins
In the wayside inn
Of his Rubaiyat dream?
"Before the phantom
Of False morning died
Methought a Voice
Within the Tavern cried,"
He heard that voice!
And he was ready,
But the insight ran rapidly away
Like a frightened rat,
Into the oblivion
Of an over-defined world.

Or should he just go back to sleep
And hope to remember the goadings
Of his muse come first light?
But, of course, he seldom does,
And his greatest poem is gone,
Like Kubla Khan on his mountain top,
But no one mourns what never was.
In the nagging fog of lost inspiration
He ends up losing on all counts
And has to wonder what verse
Is worth this torture? Perhaps
All of it. That's the answer.

farther, faster

To write is to run, faster,
To run ahead of endings and regret,
Writing to get the poem
Behind the writer
So he can move farther, because
Every poem is an anchor
Of indecision till it's done,
If it ever can be done. Yes,
This is a subject of debate,
For every poem tends to generate
Revisions and divisions
In fusioning and fissions.
Think of the cone of the upstart universe
Inflating after the bang
Into so much mindless chatter,
And here the metaphor gets further
Mixed—explosion, road, water, flower.
To finish the work is to cut the rope,
The fuse, the stem, to break the chain,
What holds fast against the current,
So the river of inspiration
Might carry him to sea
Or space or time unknown,
Wherever satisfaction waits
In new lines, new tongues, tempers
And fresh contradictions.

new years eve

He went to Times Square on New Years Eve
To relive a memory of community,

Only to find too much light, too many people,
And every individual caged,

Not one drunk of the Wine of the Sun (a new ordinance).
Instead, a sadness stalks and pervades.

Then truth struck—this malaise was not theirs,
It was his own. He was no longer young!

He'd been a traveler here, long ago,
When the world was raw with wild flowers.

People fought, drank, but their pain and joy were shared.
There was everything to look forward to,

Life was always beginning,
Every tableau tasted of colors to come.

And so, as travelers do, he returned
In elder years, researching that past he imagined,

Dragging the black sack of envy and misunderstanding,
Plus the rusted rebar and broken bricks of memories.

But the happiness of others disturbed him,
The madness of crowds he could not longer share.

He just could not get past the barricade, into the living,
Where he longed to sing, but never had,

Until he spied the reason—at the far end of 42nd street,
A high-masted ship at the East River sat,

Awaiting embarkation,
Waiting to ferry him from every sorrow.

The Reaper's Flag was raised, the loading ramp
Was empty and no provisions crowded that deck

But a pile of brown skulls to be used in canons
To conquer the new, resistant lands of tomorrow.

bone frame radio

He has always claimed to be cold,
Cold as a doused fire or frozen bones
Unearthed near the poles,
And when he's buried,
His stripped down cold radio frame
Will draw remote signals
From outer realms, new and old,
And send them back to space the same.
The signals stay in play for ages,
After frost fades from the globe,
After ice melts from the glaciers,
And the warm seas swell.
And the dead zones here,
And barren exo-planets there,
Spinning far from the sun, and all
The dirty snow and stone
Of insentient nature
Will resonate with riddles
And pointed transmissions,
In thorns of fire, in needles of light,
In poison spears of declarations.
They leave the organic body
Unencumbered, seeking ears on far stars
And mind in a mute universe.
They leave as pleas of those
In death's chains: "We once lived!
Their signals sing,
"Come discover what remains
Of the sacrifice we made
In the service of our fame."

hard sleep

They may wake on rocky beds
By river or sea, where their migrant mind drives them,

Soaked in hard rain and tears, or they may wake
On forest floors, sleeping kits wrapped in holy fire,

Or they may rise like hungry ghosts on highway sides
As semis thunder past in company of runners, escapees,

Or in patches of grass and sunflowers, where they slept rough
With bee stings, biting ants, nagging crows and barnyard hens.

They may wake in strange beds beside unnamed lovers,
Or alone along edges of many an uncomfortable abyss.

Some sleep like tragic heroes, pens in their fists,
Nails in their palms, on green hillsides in foreign climes.

Some sleep in love's armor, some in soft clothes, under
Newspaper blankets, on pillows of gravel, road dust and bone.

Some bed down on paving stones or subway grates, or late
At night in graveyard plots with restless shades of the lost.

It was never easy, this life, but always sublime,
In the solitude of the forbidden, in the heartless noose of time.

And many a poet, on reaching the end of their writer's rope,
Wakes far from shore, riding that fateful outbound tide,

With the moon at full, cold and high,
While back on land left far behind, siren songs and cries arise

Of those still roaming earth in verse, with a gallows stride,
Searching for their resting place, ready to die.

no river, no foot

Part 1
The raindrop formed
In atmospheric conflict,
Strikes earth, sublimates
Then ceases to exist,
But the soak, splatter, splash
Of it speeds along,
Collects in tiny streams
That hyper happy children ride
Flashing jazz hands
And slapping knobby knees,
As they hop, leap and skip
All babble and trick,
Impermanence makes the ride
Bubbly, audacious,
And mass times gravity,
Keeps it rapacious
In the flight to dependents
Of deep wells and holes
While fighting the flood gate's
Effort to control,
Fighting at the faucet valve's
Measure of its flow.
Behold the tidal wave states
Indifferent and so rolling
From the throttled melt
Of mountain snow
To sour mash barrel
And the brown liquor bottle.
Grand Rios of whisky, Volgas of wine
Rivers of legend and rivers of time
Great Gangas and Danubes,
Colorados and Congos,
Blue Niles and Ohios.
Tall tales will be told
Of Seines and Mississippis,
And drinking songs sung
Of Amazons and Mekongs,
Yangtzes and Yukons,
Roman Tibers of legend
And Turinese Pos,

The water harps of many Arps,
And singing Russian Dons.
The mind scores a musical
Of umbrellas and rain,
Watersheds and veins,
And blood turned to ink
By ecstasy and pain
Expressed under pressure
When the poet overthinks
Penning thoughts in a drunk,
Getting bloated or impatient
And pissing wild visions
Down the kitchen sink.

Part 2
Oh, where is the Mike Fink
Of the coronary arteries
Where the Mark Twain
Of the minor capillaries?
Every body is a frontier
For legend and for fable.
As our mythic debt is great
To gravitation's dictates
Of atom to molecule
To cloud to rain
To ocean to cell
To body to brain,
Then back to endless rain,
Where we claim
Our place in the flow, or try,
Though doomed to fail,
For this is how and why
That story will go,
This is the journey
Of the poet's holy road:
You never set foot in the same river twice.
You never set foot in the same river once.
You never even set a solid foot.
You never even are
A single "You" really,
Neither foot nor step,

No river, no motive, no need,
No telos, no arc,
No "supposed to be";
No, the Self is a construct
Escaping all frames,
For newer containers,
And disparate names,
You are like to the water
Whose path to both tower
And temporary flower
Is equal to the opposites—
Submission and power.

excavations of intimacy

"Come, butterfly
It's late-
We've miles to go together."

memory theater

Memories of this city ask for maps
Both inhospitable and magnetic,
Calling yet warning: "Watch your back!"
Beware the traces:

Complex routes marked by stick-pins.
Connected with threads of past habits
Hung with post-it notes—a laundry
Line of the worn and once hidden.

Buildings arrive fully loaded,
Events taped off like crime scenes
On sidewalks leading with haloed footprints,
Exit routes in a doomed plane.

Memory waits at odd corners,
A mugger with a knife, blackjack and gossip,
Waiting to reanimate old pain
And polish the bruise.

Is it really appropriate to honor the missing
Like this, in Ars Memoriae via Manhattan?
Such an exercise in self-indulgence
Is something she'd disapprove of,

Yet it keeps her vibrant in this indifferent city
She loved, but did not love her back,
Where unnoticed, she put in her earthly hours
With drive and marvelous conviction.

mappa mundi

The refrigerator surface
Was covered with notices
Of political organizations,
Photos of nieces, grand landscapes,
Phone numbers, flyers, reminders
For concerts, plays, post cards,
All held in a shifting cartography
By equally symbolic magnets

That functioned as nodes,
Wind monsters, compass roses, maelstroms.
I could use them to connect currents,
Latitude and longitude lines
Into continents, islands, lone lighthouses
On oceans of interests and obligations
And know something of who she was,
Where she'd been and would go.

A vast enamel ice sheet
Underlay that confused map,
And I could hear the compressor
Of the great indifferent appliance
Beneath our human activity
And know it for its bounty,
For I could open the door that held
The fantastic cartography of her life
And make a lunch from the leftovers.

east 3rd street

It was East 3rd Street
Where we first met and spoke in the stairwell
At the gallery where she was employed.
The time I held her was there at Tribes—
She was upset. She didn't know me.
We'd hardly spoken. But I felt comfortable..
Later I would be accused, by cynics
Of hitting on a vulnerable woman, snaking my arm
Around her waist with bad intention.

Once, I saw her walking west on E. 3rd
Coming from the bus stop at Ave D.
Despite determination, she was always late.
I thought to shout, but a self-destructive instinct
Stopped me, a hesitation I came to regret.
She might have liked to hear me call her name.

Not long after, at a block party on East 3rd.
She was selling vintage clothes.
I circled her table like a teenager with a crush.
Would she like to see Hair at the Delacorte?
I asked. She said sure, trying to be casual.
The next day I stood for two hours
But they cut off the line just before my turn.
When I told her, she didn't care.
She was only glad I tried,
Sensing the start of a greater story.

1st ave

I saw her walking up 1st Ave one night
I guess around 10th or 11th.
We had only recently started dating.
It was surprising to see her
On the street in her "other" life.
And I remember thinking
"There she is! What will I say?
Will she be glad to see me?"
I didn't know. I doubt she did either.
Later, I would know better her routes
And how to avoid them.
She didn't like being disturbed
In her travels, even by me.
She had priorities, after all.

bedford ave

The Salvation Army on N. 7th
Had a once-a-week, half-price day.
I ran into her a couple of times
As I was often in that neighborhood.
She was a little put off.

We both had rituals, after all,
It was a duty to maintain distance.
We did go together once or twice
But she could spend hours in a thrift store
Where I was a quick scan.

That store's long gone now.
The area has grown upmarket, hi-tech,
Artisanal and decidedly unthrift,
But I can still see her amongst the racks,
Browsing the shelves of bric-a-brac.

The streets care little for our memories,
As I imagine Baudelaire, sipping a latte
And scribbling in some hipster café:
"Old Brooklyn no longer exists! Alas,
The city changes faster than the human heart."

I too think of that homesick swan in exile,
Amongst neighborhoods turned to allegories,
Gnawed by longing, ridiculous, sublime,
Hypocrite lecteur! mon semblable, mon frère!
Why search for what we'll never find?

florescence

Some people shine in artificial light
And she was one: the Indian buffets
Of Murray Hill, Dojos on 4th, Baskin Robbins,
Big Daddy's on Park South.

We treasured the strange hyper-caloric
Forbidden iHop confections of 14th St.
Her eyes lit up in the Houston St. ice cream parlor
Even though she always got peanut butter.

Despite the cuisine or class of the place
Her joy was the process of deciding,
Though she always ordered the same thing,
Thinking she hadn't before.

Expressions of pleasure appeared
Above her head in cartoon balloons,
Dipping her fork into the mess and mixing
Everything together like kids do.

She didn't eat fast and seldom finished,
So we'd have it wrapped to go,
But waffles and pancakes have no second life,
And tempura vegetables cannot be revived.

Nan gets moldy,
Curried vegetables get soggy, fries get rubbery.
Styrofoam trays sat in the fridge for days,
Remembering old auras of florescent light.

I didn't care where we ate or if we finished.
My joy was sitting with someone
Who spoke to the servers with kindness,
And always remembered their names.

---

la vita nuova

1)
Late evenings I might come home
From some big city ego-driven game,
To find her outside, waiting for me
Waiting for help to carry her bags.

I'd learn she'd been out front
For some time—standing there
With that monk-like patience that always
Drove me crazy and a little jealous.

To her it was okay to stand in place,
Examine one's thoughts and watch the world,
"To just exist" she would say, because
Someday you won't, and won't know this.

2)
Against the rage of gentrification—
We pursued a smaller, closer life.
Reading aloud in that room: Dante,
Shaw, Wilde, and New Yorker cartoons.

We did our laundry in the bathtub,
Dried clothes on cabinet knobs, curtain rods.
Piles of books formed unstable towers
Which often fell in the night.

We never had a table, not even a chair,
And took our meals, not facing, but beside
Each other, on the edge of our bed,
Knocking spoons and touching foreheads.

3)

One time she came home drunk.
She was never drunk, but she'd stayed
Too long at some gallery event, lost track
And was embarrassed for it.

One time her hair caught fire on the stove.
I wasn't home. She ran into the hall.
But the neighbors did not open their doors
And the smell lingered for days.

Many events arrange themselves
For recognition, like cards in a fortune spread.
Did you pay attention? Each asks,
Did you fully exist? I can only say I tried.

4)

Then came the new beginning,
Followed by difficult days. Those easy
Quotidian joys grew tense with panic.
And "Just Being" was a gamble with failure.

Then came the time when walking circles
On the roof was the best she could do,
So determined she was. I walked beside,
Holding her arm to keep her upright.

Then came the time she wouldn't come
Home again to our small, precious life.
What she needed I was not equipped to give.
Shamefully, I felt some relief at this.

5)
And now the apartment is empty
Despite bags and shelves stuffed full
With books and thrift store finds,
Flyers and stacks of unwashed dishes.

Now is the new life of endless nights
Sitting on the edge of the bed we shared,
Eating simple dinners in silence,
Glancing to the space she once filled,

"And you will miss this," the voice repeats,
Too late aware of what has passed,
Faithful to a future that promises nothing,
While blind to the present of living.

brush ridge road

Sometimes consciousness is a Theremin
Played by unseen hands from afar.
I felt this from all the differing forms
I could covet and stay with the music,
As over the arc of a single crescendo,
I learn through the eyes of avatars:

Summer fawn, red fox, salamander
Bear cub, ground hog and jay—
Their eyes watch the sky for a sign.
These forms become possible to me
As bridges by which I might find her,
Like a child delights in the butterfly wing
Or a monk in the stopped clock of mind.

I came to search every crevice and fold
Of the world as concrete and representation,
Knowing that, when searching for omens,
One finds them, searching for us.
Life opens many hands as extensions
Be it the prickly fingers of a spruce,
Or the cold metal of a lawn chair's arm,

Such hands grant an overfull animate world,
Made so precisely because she has gone.
And because nothing is ever truly done
But is always in process, the wake
Of departure leaves a void that wants filling.
Buckets of rain and harvest horns spilling
Ripe berries, dandelions, daisies,

All shout: There is promise in grief!
Look only to the rising tide of tongues,
Eyes and shapes she has taken to speak.
But will she approve of her audience?
This old fool obsessed with phantoms,
Chasing yellow butterflies on the morning lawn,
Hoping to capture what's already gone.

visiting hours

I always bring something
We can share, like a sandwich,
A chocolate muffin or cranberry scone.
She liked peanut butter cups best,
So I carry the bite-sized kind
In my pocket and we have a picnic.
I press her portion into the earth,
Pour out a splash of favored beverage
And knock on her stone like we used to
Knock spoons before our meals,
Because I like to imagine down there,
Her yellow bones are famished,
And her dried tongue craves refreshment
And that she smiles, if she can without lips,
As the fare trickles deeper in the earth
With each rain, each mist,
And that she thinks of me on the surface,
Passing what life is left as best I can.
Does she feel my physicality,
The gravity of my mind,
And think my sorrow too heavy
For her fragile frame to bear?
Or is my burden welcome,
Like a weighted blanket providing
Comfort and containment
For the long cold night she abides.

lapis lazuli

Lapis lazuli as a stone
Signals no fixed place.
Embarkation and destination
Can't be found,
Nor any frame of time,
For what's contained
In the cloud and star-strewn
Skies and midnight oceans
Are vaults of possibility,
But no secure horizon
Or handle to hold.

The traveler, mapless,
Stands or floats past lands
And seas that can't be known,
To the undead end
Of roads and plans,
Facing the thrill of the threshold,
Where marsh and moor
And the racing planes of mythic shores
Meet unbound tides.
Water and sky collide
But fail to close on a line.
There's no lighthouse to guide.

And so,
Being wonder's pilgrim as she was,
Lapis was her favorite gem,
And over the years,
I brought her such charms
As hoped could hold her:
A lapis ring of cobalt blue
A scooped cerulean worry stone,
A bracelet of Curacao beads,
An amulet of speckled blue pearl
Wrapped in silver filigree
And I still have these.

A dark blue heart
Freckled with gold,
Caught my eye in a curio shop
On a grey quaint lane
Of the Paris Marais.
I bought that pendant
And carried it home
Wrapped in blue cotton
For her birthday in May,
But in the end,
With no other choice
I buried that heart at her grave.

Perhaps it feeds her,
Directs her dreams
Through the endless days,
While I carry its sibling,
A mirror of kind,
A pocket mate, a blueberry kiss,
An oval, an egg,
A sister transmitter
To receive and sustain
Those plans we made
For our rendezvous
Beyond this mortal plane.

For it's true!
As poets are wont to say,
Eternity can be
Activated between one's fingers
Like a small coin
That has no other value
But to join, at least in the mind,
Those parted in body,
Untethered in time.

pickup truck

The truck was no fixed location, but a beast of passage —
Low slung, underpowered, a driveway clothes rack,

Starship and 4-cylinder Conestoga wagon
For a shrunken America, in which we rode from

Route 28 to 87 to elsewhere, Baltimore to the Adirondacks,
New Jersey to New Kingston and on, we drove

To the dumps of Delaware County, past Roxbury rapids,
Waterfalls of Catskill Xanadus,

Past endless yard sales of the mortgage dispossessed,
Through the boarded-up streets of bypassed America.

Out of the flood zones and derelict towns, we drove,
Victorian thrift store hobos doing road karaoke,

Singing Hank and Johnny, Monteverdi and Bo Diddley.
In the midst of mystery, mapless, without GPS, we drove,

Pulling to the shoulder for thunderstorms and white-out blizzards,
Changing drivers at truck stops,

Small-time usurpers at the vessel bridge, gazing wild-eyed
Through Nautilus windows at the Void Space of the Now

Where the radiant octopus arms of street lights slid down
Undersea hillsides, and the flaming roads threw forth phantoms.

The lighted bestial grasshoppers of the night highways
Trucked their cargo to unknown ports.

It could have all been ours, and it was,
Though our biggest trip was no further than the front yard

Where we hosted tailgate parties for two,
Drank Mexican lager, snacked on smoked salmon, water crackers,

Watched the crows, hawks, foxes, and other neighbors
Watching us watching the slow weeds and wildflowers grow.

—

And at night we lay on the reflective black truck hood
As it made two skies to contain us,

And we floated between them, bed and ceiling,
Between meteor showers and cold automotive steel,

Cold in our coats like frail astronauts in hurling tin cans,
Bathing in the turbulent air of the universe.

And, after all this exploration, we'd return to the mundane city,
Flying south on the FDR Drive,

That rollicking race track down the Eastside,
Then I'd drop her off on Grand St in front of the Rite Aid,

And she'd head uptown to work while I looked for a parking space
On the grey streets of Brooklyn.

spider and arrow

I don't remember exactly when or where
The spider plant first appeared—
Maybe Portland, maybe Chicago.
It had been with me for 45 years,
15 apartments and 2 cross-country car trips.

Now it lives in the shower stall window
Of my downtown studio. And let me tell you,
It has suffered. I've dumped the whole ecosystem
On the floor and had to remake it. I've starved it
Of water for weeks, yet it survives.

Once I noticed foreign leaves growing
Among the spider vines and pulled them,
Thinking them to be invading weeds.
She was quite angry when she found out,
For they were her plantings.

So of course, I replanted. Here, five years
After her passing, those arrowhead vines flourish.
Unlike the old spider, who's known such tragedy
And negligence, the new comers
Are wild, wanting, young and hungry.

The plants co-exist for now, woven together
In a potted mess I can no longer separate.
But I want both survive, so after I'm gone,
Someone might nurture this living memorial
To two beings once so knotted in their bonds
They made one organism.

dead trees

It's an odd association,
But when I see winter trees on the road
Or in gray fields forming black patterns
Like fugitives from abstract paintings
I'm reminded of the shadows of her hands.

We had similar hands, she and I—
Scrawny long fingers, lumpy knuckled,
With oft unkempt nails,
And we both had big veins.
Junkies would love our veins.

And just as the naked hungry trees
Were art for me, so were her fingers,
Though not delicate or fine,
It was the quality of their touch,
That stumbling, hesitant exploration
Of wisdom gained in humility.

Her hands were the books that held books,
Histories that told history,
But anxious hands do nervous things—
They wring, pick lint, scratch scabs,
Pull cuticles and draw blood.
I tried to stop that when I could.

The willow in my yard died the next year—
A sympathetic act, perhaps.
But I still refuse to cut it down.
I love the artful curl of the limbs
Forming cups for stars, arches that frame
The moon in its passing.

They remind me of the arc of her arm at night,
Reaching for me in sleep, and how
I pulled that hand close, hoping our veins
Like rivers would combine, even knowing
They already had before we met.

mona lisa at rest

She did not dream like me
Not with restless anxiety, in lucid tales,
Or claustrophobic night sweats gained
Through inner movie plots
Of endless pursuit, no,
Her dreams were quiet, she claimed,
And the proof was in the smile
She maintained, no matter
What hour of night or morning
I looked at her—a Mona Lisa-like
Moon sliver of contentment
Settled on her lips, and I could
Stare at that resting face for hours.
It was nurture, it was energy,
And it helped me believe some peace
Was possible on the other side.
I know she fought for that smile,
It had been a long struggle to win,
And I was glad she never woke to catch me
Stealing some of that victory as my own.
She might have thought I was weird,
Like the creepy dude who sits
In the dark corner of the bedroom
In the horror films we loved to watch,
Waiting for the innocent
Victim to wake up.

the archeologist

As archeologist of the small,
I work with the most delicate tools
On a past of singular import.
Now I'm at a dig of a fragile sort,
Unearthing the culture
Of a vast civilization of one,
Dusting off artifacts—
The corroded rivets, ropes and jewels
That held two worlds in a net,
And sadly coming to realize
How much better I know her,
Now that she's gone,
Knowing as well there are two
Kinds of knowing to the quest:
The intuition of presence,
Which is that of the moment,
And the other of evidence,
Pointing deep in the past.
And so I keep at both
With my brushes, spoons,
And magnifying glass,
Believing the truth of her
Is bigger than any city,
Country or culture,
Bigger than any Pompey,
Atlantis, Aztec or Incan Empire,
More expansive by many kingdoms
Than Saxon ships had pillaged,
Buried now in mounds,
More lucrative than foreign ports
Served by merchant traders
Sunken now to the sea floor,
But it's also true
That all these facets and facts
Have only come to light
Because of the storm, the quake
The catastrophic crack
In the world that brought to the surface
What had not been revealed
Until, of course, one survivor
Went looking for it.

—

black hole

The disc of a CD spins
Around its black hole
Like a captured galaxy
Titled "Her Voice"
With a marking pen.
The disc holds phone calls
Recorded as MP3 files
Collected and burnt
In digital code—
Dozens of messages
In varying degrees
Of desperation, declaration,
Requisition and desire.
It's an aural archive covering
Several hard years,
And I like to think of them
As conversations pressed in wax,
Like back-in-the-day,
Something I could spin on a turntable
In some crackly tableaux
Of a life long ago.

There's a critique
To be made of this vision:
I've always been obsessed
With the concept of vortices—
Things, objects spinning
Around dense nothing,
Into which, if you fell,
You'd never come back
From the event horizon,
The annihilating grip,
So I never play the messages,
Because once I start that galactic
Ride to the inner abyss,
Once I become lost like that,
I won't be able to contemplate
The very voice I saved,
Nor the reason for the saving,
Nor her position in space,

Nor would I remember her in time
As the animated being I loved,
And if those memories are lost,
Then that much of her as lives in me
Will be lost as well,
And it's my job to keep her in play,
Even if it means not actually playing
The music anymore.

place saint sulpice

I was wandering through an antique
Book market in Place Saint Sulpice,
Vaguely looking for a gift,
When I found a monograph
Of butterfly photographs
With commentary by Collette.
It would be a great addition to her collection
Of books on the subject,
Remembering how she watched
These fairy beings
With great fascination
In our yard upstate.
She had several delicate balsam-wood
Butterfly sculptures, tchotchkes really,
That she'd placed around,
On shelves and mantles,
But I was always moving them
Because they got in the way
And I was afraid they'd break,
Besides they seemed out of context
Given the darkness of the place.
She was sort of angry with me
About my lack of regard,
And I really regret giving her a hard time,
I didn't know how much they meant,
So I put them back.
Perhaps they'll attract her spirit
And I can look forward to seeing her
In the butter yellow wings,
Of her avatars again,
When spring brings wildflowers.
And the search for nectar
Arouses desire across the land.

body of bliss, heart of light

When I met her
I never suspected
What a furious dancer she was,
But I danced with her

At weddings, parties,
Outdoor concerts,
And if a public were to judge,
We danced like agents of destruction.

Normally I wouldn't
Dance like that,
But she brought it out of me,
Like a prism brings out the rainbow.

People often thanked us
For our crazy dancing,
Said we brought life,
To floorboards saturated with death.

At a New Years Eve party once
On the Upper West Side
We danced our asses off,
Like Parvati and Shiva making love.

Now that was some passion—
It frightened the gods.
They felt the world might come to an end
But one was born instead.

The sedate New Year's audience
Watched from the couch,
A little embarrassed
By our shameless energy.

But why should we care,
We were birthing a universe of our own,
And they were probably afraid
It could swallow them.

crushes

It's odd how
After she was gone
Guys who nursed crushes
On her through the years
Became known to me.
They came out of the paneling
Like waiting shades,
Out of old letters and postcards,
Emails and portraits,
Each with a politic and history.
Some were long-haired,
Reticent or vicarious lovers
Living in basements,
Some in suburbs.
They rose like ghosts
In a gallery of repressed desires
Not saying anything specific
About their claims on her,
Though it was obvious
Enough to make me realize
Just how lucky I was
To have won her
In such a crowded field,
And I wonder if she knew that,
If she knew how
As heir to her afterlife largess
I felt like a bastard prince
Who did not deserve
And never did earn
His place at the table.

flailing

The connection has been lost
And we're out there now,
Floating on our own
In the immensity
Of the fallen lives we live
Now, and going forward,
Squabbling over the scraps
Of fame or simple dignity,
Selling mediocrity by brand name,
And I think of how she fought
Against this poison tide
In her imperfect, impassioned way,
And did so never for her own glory
But for the sake of an elusive justice,
The freedom of peoples and species,
The healing of the planet and psyches,
And maybe she always was
Just treating depression with activity
And regret with duty,
But it was never an act.
It wouldn't have worked so well
If it was.

barrel fire songs
and back-alley ballads

"Bitten by fleas and lice,
I slept in a bed,
A horse urinating all the time
Close to my pillow."

highway 61 revisited

The day I was born they told me I was dead,
Everything blue turned out to be red,
Whatever was worst was the best they said,
As they planted little devils in the back of my head.

My school teacher told me that I had no brain,
So I went to the courthouse to change my name,
Discovered my landlord was really my father,
And that pretty little lover, she was really my daughter.

Told my sister don't marry nobody named John,
There was some kind of lie I promised my mom,
Bought a can of pork and beans and some chewing gum,
Had change left over for a six-pack and a gun.

So I went to a bank, but I thought it was a bar,
Showed the clerk my muzzle then I borrowed a car,
Ran every red light in the city square,
I drove real fast but I went nowhere.

I ate a bitter pill from a woman untrue,
Drank the oldest whiskey from the fountain of youth,
What seemed like kindness was really cruel,
Nothing was ancient, everything was brand new.

Out there the country looks exactly like the town,
The sky very strangely looks exactly like the ground,
Staring at the world through a cracked windshield,
Where the truth is a lie and the lies are too real.

At home on my computer screen, I'm told I'm having fun,
But it's not really home, I'm really on the run,
The next door neighbor's just another road bum,
And this dirty asphalt carpet is my Highway 61.

Sold my soul at the crossroads, still my axe wont tune,
But my brain pan fries in the cybernetic sun.

hiroshima mon amour

These days are a string of repeating April Fools,
A hedonistic dance beneath the Reaper's sickle moon,
The 4th of July, that day of our founding,
Found us with no sane place to belong.

So I checked into the Anxiety Arms Hotel,
I tried to get some rest but the media was raising hell,
I had a sweet dream that I was already dead,
But woke up with a vacuum cleaner hose stuck in my head.

So I went down to join the Human Pride Parade,
But everybody there was either drunk or getting paid,
While over at the Haymarket Shopping Mall,
A demonstration for peace became a bourgeois brawl.

Some said it was a new Populist Revolution,
The free market commodified propaganda and pollution,
Desire and justice struck a backroom deal,
While the Nouveau Riche built a digital Bastille.

So I sought refuge in the old Global Village,
But all the news on TV was about rape and pillage,
I asked an economist what the hell was going on,
He said Das Capital was a brand new kind of bomb.

Gossip passed as truth, the facts were passed as lies,
The courts became the place where human rights were sent to die,
Beggars can't be choosers in the game of imitation,
The end of the world seemed like a possible solution.

Now, all the prophets sing Hiroshima Mon Amour,
Facebook drops the Fat Boy, the wasteland breeds the war,
Narcissistic greed is bringing everybody down,
And our world leaders have become Insane Clowns.

It was the Summer of No Love in the Season of Descent,
In this fractured lonely Country of Our Discontent,
I began with the ideals of a brash newcomer,
But my moral bank could never pay the rent.

Still, sometimes I think it might be nice
To measure our days in pleasure and pain,
But the road ahead will never be just wrong or right,
The world should never be that simple again.

when the last thing real in the blighted field is the broke-down derelict automobile

Mushroom clouds pop like sticky hot rolls,
Broccoli stalks smoke off cranial atolls,

Scythe thoughts swipe under L-train rails
As human heads bowl down the uncanny vale.

The crack of pool balls and jukebox moons,
Hubcap drum rhythms, bones and spoons,

They rise in ire like a carburetor slide,
As spin floods the ear with its toxic tide.

Spines get snapped, forging fashion nails
Pinning everyday martyrs onto Catherine wheels.

Sex machines shag down raunchy train lines
As poetic verse winds back, blank to rhyme.

And what of proof in these overstuffed times?
Six million years times relentlessness,

Wild lies spew from some pundit's paid lips,
Moral ornament rings the public fingertips.

Oh no, don't laugh! We all do this,
We all do that:

We all die in our grind-house time,
As candy colored clowns parade with sinister affect,

Fat gestures in jest, rhetorical extremes,
On the personality stage of wing-nut schemes.

Do you remember those great Shakespearean birds?
We once claimed dignity at their clawed feet.

Such a lofty arena this may not be,
As we falsify truth, flog long dead meat.

For we already live on parallel lines,
Ages away from our early lot.

Our progenitor in empathy has been forgot.
And the congress, the khans, the royal blood bonds,

They've all been forgot,
With their chins uplifted over gun-barrel digits,

OCDs and STDs,
Hips and brains of cottage cheese,

And working class stickmen trapped in a jig
Of partisan bullhorns and thousand-watt bulbs.

Living in the belly of cornucopian plenty,
The call to bare arms and disorder lives

Has all the actors swatting coffin flies
That breed beneath the stage boards

Of a porch in Disney shantytown
Where two tramp thespians differ to agree,

As they lounge on moldy sofa cushions,
Rusty coil springs,

Quenching their thirst from a brown paper sack,
Holding bottled non-conformity, brewed in duplicity,

And the sad sack semi-colon to this scene
Is the derelict auto on its axles and knees,

A trophy propped on cinder blocks,
That once drove high achievers to their deeds,

Sitting dead as a Dodo by the future's empty shed,
Wrapped in pious thorn vines and carnivore weeds.

at the vanity fair

The Ascetic left the bosom of his Meditation Pool
To drive past the habits of the squares and fools
In a rag-top Camaro with red vinyl seats
And a radio cranked to the politic beat.

He relished the epic and dressed swell for it—
His cigarette hung off a cynical lip
With sharkskin trousers draping scuffed wingtips,
Riding tidal iterations of mimetic drift.

He carried a toothbrush and a fish-rib comb
And the beat bad streets of his bliss did roam
With a cocked fedora and his heart on a spit
Beating in his ribs like a carnal drum kit.

A Romantic cad searching creeds outworn,
Miscredited, uncounseled and misinformed,
A prodigal son born of incantation
In a world, it seems, that was too much with him.

All night he wandered as the juke bands played
In neon arcades of that tripped out town,
Where vixens in their Saturday pick-up gowns
Cruised cats in their screen star shades.

And the saxophones screeched their Bebop tropes
While guitars shredded cold steel blue notes
That trumpets under wrote in brutish tones,
Then came the clamor of the wild trombones.

Somewhere the farmer trucks his field
While the hipster sucks on a hand-rolled square,
But the "here and now" all crave to purchase
Is not where they are—not then, not there.

In the grey green hours of dying night,
The long post-hours of wine blindness,
The hunters of love in their failing plight,
Swap lies for a date or a loaded kiss.

And whatever their fate was or would be,
They will muster their last lustful energy,
As ignoble thoughts curl into songs
And question marks hover over right and wrong.

The streetlamp martyrs all beg to be saved
While poorly shaven men turn in sleepless graves
And ladies of the wee hours count their gains
As the morning sheds tears of red-eyed rain.

ballad of a stage hand

Let's drink to bold mates never had,
　To times that likely never were.
Props to the actor with the put-on zeal,
　Whose progress assumes a right to steal.

His role is promotion of the profit ideal
　His hero, the traveling snake oil man
Crossing that porous moral borderland
　For a pontiff's kiss on his grifter's hand.

Behind a tack-tufted leather clad door
　In a boarded up vaudeville theater
In the dressing chamber, another masochist prays
　To a mirror of shifting character shades.

Footlights shine from the edge of the stage
　On a play of "being" but meaning nothing by it,
For who remembers the script first signed,
　The poisoned cup, the better offers declined.

Wherefrom? Whereto? By what? They pine.
　The clay, the potter or the melting pot?
All yield not, not the film still pique,
　Not the over-bleached teeth or screen-death sleep

Of sold-out souls stuffed in showbiz skins
　Waiting lost years for a changed set piece.
Let the hurdy-gurdy grind through the *longue durée,*
　Let horse hooves fry on the farrier's iron,

Nostalgia is the market, but the question is why?
　To what succumb, to how & when?
To the promise of identity given to each
　When self is nothing but a nest of speech?

Using star charts sold in market stalls,
   Scrawled by touts on salamander skins,
The future was planned and pinned to the walls
   Shortly before the world's fated end

Had already begun, or was soon to begin
   In this country of anger and fear-forged armor,
Where violence flowers in religious splendor,
   But no righteous smith of reason or faith

Could shackle or saddle the acquisitive gait
   Or take proper measure of whore or priest
Or the hunger artist choking on charms
   Of old time allures that once spurred the race on.

Are there any among us speaking dead tongues
   With advice for such as think as we?
Is there prophecy scratched on windowpanes
   Preserved as a transparent third degree?

So hale those bold friends we never had,
   And times that likely never had been.
Hale the wisdom tree's never-born fruit,
   As parasites feast on the harvest of truth,

As among new tribes, we flee and spin
   History, tragedy, dull tired puns,
And dancing by the fires of the End of Days
   Curse in rubber bullets from deep-throat guns.

Who cares to lounge night in, night out,
   The long perhaps, the increased doubt?
Forever and ever we'll impotently cry, we're lost
   To the Now and we'll never know why!

foreign born

We fled the dictators of the mind
The clerics and guards of the body
We fled our dead currency
Our failed economy
We fled the repression
We fled the oppression
We fled persecution and oversight
We fled the four horsemen
The border pens and strongmen
We left the recession and blight
We left behind poison
We left behind prison
We escaped the death state
We rejected the racism, fascism, hate
We broke social chains
Of class and self-doubt
We left behind drought
We left behind rain
We left the starvation
The class exploitation
We fled imposition, as victims of blame
We escaped from the pogroms
We ran from the wars
We left brothers and sisters
We left our ancestors
We left our possessions and friends
We crossed over the line
We crossed over the boundary
We ignored all the signs
We snuck in through customs
We crossed over oceans
We migrated across burning skies
We crossed the high mountains
And passed many checkpoints
Before we arrived
We came here like water
We came here like fire
We came out of ice and trauma and storm
We came here as seekers
We came here as teachers
We came here as leaders

As shoppers and merchants
And newspaper readers
We came here with scientific minds
We are poets and singers
Fry cooks and cleaners
Doctors and dancers and creative thinkers
Workers on bridges and railroad lines
If you look in the mirror
You'll see we are you
In a changed age and hue
For we're all foreign born
Naked, alone and searching a home
So don't close the door
You'll soon ask for more
Of our will, of our work
And our critical eye
For we are your history
Of resistance, your memory
Your body of hardship and love
We are the seed and the fruit of your tribe
Without us you will not survive
Without us no one survives.

this land is your land

Arriving on a rickety, early 20th century
NYC Train, American decline
Pulls into the station, a century behind
The modern world.

Dirty, unkempt subway cars
Filled with the homeless
Whose loud running commentaries
Are bitter, aggressive and rightly so,

Within this reality of distrust and danger,
Not to mention resentment
That lasts as many stops as you can stand it
If one survives the ride.

Emerging to the good time market streets,
You immediately notice a masked
Sadness weighting everything that moves
In this beat down, broken country,

Whose sidewalks are full of confused citizens:
Those left behind by education,
Left behind by simple dignity
Left behind by healthcare, left behind, yes,

And yet encouraged to fight,
But mostly against each other,
For the scraps Late Capital allows.
Anger is pandemic,

Everyone is special, so they've been told,
But the cult of individualism has left them
Oddly grayed out, blended and alone
In a world of false community,

So they walk their beat in bad health,
Bent and disabled,
And vaguely remembering a birthright
They missed out on,

As the country divides on conflicting moral claims,
Well there's always Netflix
And endless Award Shows
To take away the pain.

praise song for social media

There's no gifted class for the blast furnace,
No talented programs for the mines,
Though we work in the factories a hundred years,
We got no virtues to signal here.

We get that your children are brilliant and cute,
Geniuses all, with class on their side,
The best universities are guaranteed,
With scholarships written for 4-year rides.

You are what we've been trained to praise,
You are the model of race and taste,
Your friends are amazing, you're talented as hell,
The facts of your lives, as products, sell well.

You wave to us from the Facebook screen,
You wave to us from the Artist Café,
Your latest meal is a popular post,
Risotto with mushrooms and avocado toast.

Your marriage worked out for the very best,
Your job is fulfilling for all to see,
You're clever and woke and buy the best books,
Your merit is fruit on the Economic Tree.

Can life really be like that? We ask,
When Walmart hands out no gold stars,
Home is no hearth, the family is strained,
The American dream has grown twisted and stained.

We, the audience to your self-esteem,
Oil our guns while we nuke our dinners,
Knowing our lives are but comedy shows
On the TV screens of the winners.

We'll change that channel to change the view
And your world will burn, the hour is late,
Our guillotines wait for your swelled heads to roll,
Our dream is the death of the "classless" state.

___

carousel (lullaby for Burnside/1975)

(1)
Stray cats plead in human tongues, feral dogs shred roadkill hearts,
Lovers play the absurd parts their partners deal.

Our children are born to be teething, feeding,
Beasts at the grind stone wheels of their dreams

As the blued lips of soulless clerics neither preach nor inspire
Any words to redeem this act or scene,

They only add graft to verses once sung,
Now stalled out on scraps—sturm und drang, chorus and refrain

Penciled on receipts, home-made business card backs,
And lunch tickets passed

Amongst the pilgrim tribes of Burnside
Seeking grace in the inconstant stranger.

(2)
So many faces over so many rides
With grease paint mouths and kohl-ringed eyes.

While carnival animals bob and stride—
See the saddled ostrich and the fairy-tale frog,

As they go round and round, up and down,
Circling some hidden erotic rhythm,

Promoting the fantasies of men who pretend
They've escaped from the culture devouring them,

Searching for the uncanny stranger/friend,
Who drops out of sight, but reappears with a vengeance

In the shop worn seams of their shop-worn lives.
So they sit painted horses on barber-shop poles,

Holding expressions of the duped and dumb struck
So many tragic heroes hold.

—

(3)
And there was a time before all that, very long before that—
A caged, blocked time,

When the comforting odor of urinal cakes, and the upright white
Cold divan arms reached out with comfort,

Sympathy and relief, as these cavernous, cracked porcelain
Pissoirs of the old beer halls still do.

A gambler's hand passes from card trick to cue,
To bank the fateful eight, Lucky Pocket!

And the Friendly Stranger, that grim karmic prophet reminds us
To insure that nothing will happen, simply

Anticipate the feared event, a precarious balance of luck and intent,
And a lifetime of training to break.

(4)
Well Burnside, you and I must come to terms.
Your sweet smells of burning butter, hash browns, omelettes

Bubbling on steel skillets, sausage and bacon on side.
See the neck tattoo of the graveyard chef,

A cartoon griddle man with a trickster's deft wrist,
Who ladles the daily special over toast.

See the blue roses inked on the aged lover's hands,
Blurred by long years of passion,

As heat waves rise to the grease screen and fan.
See the counter lined with bottle-bloated faces,

Broken noses like tree knuckles,
And loose cheeks sagging with unshaven fruit.

But the old graft lacks juice, so the crop being poor
Will be culled later from the mission house floor.

(5)

See the jukebox in its art-deco elegance
Prepped by the gin queen from a cheap rented room

Whose hi-ball, pill bottle and hidden spike,
Signal a spiritual kinship of like to like.

And her only excuse to exist alongside
This bar-tree bough with its battered faces

Is the night's take in offers
And what they might buy, be it bread, brief peace,

Or release of her mind from the orchestra she follows,
The abattoir inside, the symphony of knives,

As the carousel turns and the market surrounds her—
An economy of exchange toward further exchange.

(6)

Cease and desist! The sideshow lawyers plead
Against Burnside's lure and false promise,

While it's proud-chested can-can lines of whores, hustlers,
And bar-stool cowboys

Stumble into noon, into night, into dawn,
Singing Yippe Yi Yay and Fuck You Brother,

'Round rock candy campfires down by the river.
Where cold stars mingle with traffic lights.

Outside the nightclub called Jackdaw's Paradise,
Outside Big Johnson's Bar and Grill, it's long past closing

As they wait upon fruit trucks to ride to the fields
For a rooming house dollar and a blue plate meal,

Waiting for an authentic savior to shield them
From a faith they may state but willfully misplace.

---

(7)

Oh Mother, let us pray to this impotent savior,
The enfant terrible of a traffic island cross,

Who oversees our perp walk to the vanishing point,
Who laughs at the futures we've gambled and lost.

Some paw rosaries, some suck prayer beads,
Others huddle by trash can fires for warmth.

Perhaps to escape! But no, Burnside,
You've got us now, for awhile at least.

As the rollers down at the labor pool claim—
You cannot break this street across your knee, Chief,

Not like an ornery child we'd assume to teach
A lesson in bootstrap American survival,

We might break the very spleen
That has weaned and still feeds us.

(8)

Let's try to imagine the conversations here—
They speak some pact all agreed on once, but can't pin down.

The sly grin betrays the ventriloquist clown
With his fist up the puppet's backside.

Here the neon doubles in the wet concrete,
Here little magic burns the air,

As we march to the penny whistle tune and silver tongue—
You know the one.

See us in the carousel windows, grinning out to the line,
As the Friendly Stranger grins with us,

Pulling the lever on another long ride, he lingers a moment
Before crushing our ticket in his indifferent fingers.

—

requiem from the main stem

So when I die, please wrap my bones
In a burlap sack and tie it up with twine
Use pallet boards and reclaimed nails
To craft my cradle for the final ride.

Then place it on a coffin bier
Of aged and painted oak.
Please braid the wheels with highway vines
And circus rigger's rope.

Then dress a mule in a frayed straw hat
To draw me down the street
Pick daisies from the graves of fools
To dress my cart-mule's feet

Let hobos sport their priestly cloaks,
May stray dogs don crepe paper crowns
Let my dirge be sung by an aging queen
In a tattered Broadway gown

At every bar my casket calls
There'll be no cause to mourn
But a table spread with traveler's fare
Will nourish them for future storms.

Let whisky flow to turn love bold,
Steel refugees for further strife,
Let them whom I have never met
Fashion tales of my unknown life.

And if no one seems to know me,
Do not be surprised. For I stood watch,
Without face or name, like a ghost
In the corners of their eyes.

They saw me in the windowpanes
Of towns they once passed through.
I stood with them on remote roads,
Our boot soles split, our egos bruised.

They heard my footsteps follow them
In solitude through hard years.
I spoke to them from tavern mirrors.
We drank our fill of bitter tears.

We shared a drink for mystery,
We shared a drink for shame
We watched the times roll by the way
On empty streets with pointless names.

I slept with them on highway sides,
Stained with blood and spilled out wine.
I asked advice at crossroad lights,
Where martyrs hung from traffic signs.

Tell them all my life I'm hanging on,
Tell them all my life I'm cold,
I came and went without comment.
My chains were dreams, those dreams were sold

random scenes from silent film scripts

"Do not seek to follow
In the footsteps of the wise;
Seek what they sought."

armonia

1

For some time I realized she was sister
To many stock characters in works by our beloved painter:
Astronomer, alchemist, explorer, weaver of super strings,
Backwater boat captain on rain forest tributaries.
Our barn was her workshop, a Cho/Varo museum
Filled with the bounty of mystical thrift store trips
And long days salvaging the carnival roads.

2

My job in this was to write the novel of our romance
Using only birdsong to tell it, but the keyboard
Of the old Underwood had no such notes.
It was numerical only and culturally obscure,
So the narrative was constructed in strung-out equations,
Corresponding to positions and vibrations of the stars
That wandered with us as we moved through time.

3

It all made perfect sense, until the machine itself,
On which I wrote, unfolded into several shelves,
Like a tackle box filled with lures and curios,
For all language had been reduced to its original form
As small objects, those items which had always
Served to narrate the world into being
Like game pieces on the chess board of creation—
A secret hoarders and collectors know and keep.

4

A white laminate cabinet glistens with dew water
In our makeshift office under the front yard apple boughs.
I carry it inside to find it holds a collection of tools:
Small flashlights, compasses, jack knives, scopes, and weights,
Devices used to take soundings from the imaginations
Of passersby, by which one might calculate
The value of human pilgrimage.

5

There is, as well, a bag of tiny fossils in the cabinet,
And small stiff brushes and polish.
I carry these to Therese, who loves detailed engagement.
But she is preoccupied, sitting on the floor by a table,
Brushing out the flutes of clam shells that the lost
Pilgrims of Compostela pile outside our door
Every morning before breakfast. She will sort them
By color, form and level of commitment.

6

One morning I notice something shining in the yard
A Kabba-shaped, aqua-blue translucent block
Mined from the fossil beds of cosmic origin stories.
I hold it to the sky and filter the day into flavors.
Life gladly adapts itself to the lens.
Forest leaves are transformed into a school
Of iridescent fish swarming in circles around
Those nodes that hold reality in the trap of reason.

7

This block clones others like alien space ships landing
In different corners of our lives. One sits on her table,
Clear Lucite containing the small skeleton
Of an early cretaceous ancestor to the primitive embrace.
There are fish swimming around its jeweled ribs.
Fish seem to be a theme here. Then the phone rings!
Anxiously we ask ourselves why and why now?
But not to whom they belong or if we should return them.

8

Instead, we will keep these vessels for fertility's sake.
For this cabinet can generate more treasures and keys,
And as I hand the newest, most intricate key to her, the one
Fashioned in the scrollwork of her ancestral clan,
It occurs to me that this habitat of exploration
Provides her with the perfect home to occupy
Her focus for eternity, where I will join her in time.

9

And together with brushes of finest elephant hair,
Borrowed from the paint boxes of Alchemy and Sorrow,
We'll clean the amber microscope slides
Where the scenes of our lives are held in suspension.
Using many lenses, we'll release the message hidden there,
Explore the palimpsest in all its plasma, pabulum and marrow
As we live and die in a tableau of Remedios Varo.

10

Then, just as I'm about to leave this represented world
For my physical life, and free my love to her fascinations,
She shouts from the cluttered workroom,
"Dearest, I've found it, I've found the Pearl!
And, having released it from its bondage in brushstrokes,
She asks me to carry it until my return. I still have it!
It sings in my pocket like the fiery eye, by which
Spirit seekers light their path through the dark.

shift workers in the rêverie factory

1

A conversation heard one night,
Devolved to a slowed down scream.
He spent the following untold miles
And hours of chosen solitude
Searching for the source of it—
Crawling around the grey arcane
Ventilation ducts and pipes of mind,
Bending his clay in shapes to meet
Demands of a perilous fate.
But looking ahead, he just retreats
To the marsh's edge, the muddy beach,
And the lungfish stage of his personal story,
Where living clay tests potential,
Moving from sea to land and back
Evolved on tracks of muscled waves
And tides of a pre-human history,
A progress he could never entirely know
Nor ignore, nor outgrow.

2

Up smaller and smaller stairs he crawled
On narrower paths through thicker walls,
Seeking higher floors, hidden alcoves,
And arcane books in private stalls,
Till he arrived in his own kitchen
Forty years older than when he began.
But he wrote off the loss
To a worthwhile cause,
And called it a life well imagined.
What else could his vanity do?
All dance floors mask a killing floor,
The waltz of desire is a funeral jig,
Each window jamb an organ stop
In a housebound hymn of joy and pain.
There may be those who've never seen
Raw colors of the day, he thought,
But they have felt the spleen out there
And they have heard the rain.

3

An operator heard a similar scream.
And thought it might be human,
Perhaps a hundred score or more
Louder and more shrill than any
Scream he'd ever heard before,
Be it in relief or peace or war,
But when he tried to break the news
He met anger from the multitudes
Who made their case:
"We The Living, this abstract race,
Have no faith in any thing
To which we have attached our fate.
We depend on "it" but don't believe,
So we feed on a sweet black
Cloud of Unknowing to claim our sleep.　　　　,
But one man's sleep is another's hard day
At the handles of machines
Where peace cannot be bought with pay.

4

A night shift worker heard it too,
As scrambled signals strayed for years
Reassembled on his screen
In a prophecy that what's been lost
Could be something found again.
So this is the message he ran down
From the mountainside at the edge of town,
From the factories in their solitude,
He held the tablets high and cried
"The Last Act of the Tragedy.
Will be restaged for all to see."
But the mobs, preferring ignorance,
Rose in ire and accusation.
To blame the messenger is normal,
Dismiss the piper's tune!
The wound of the world will never heal,
The poison just gets passed around.
No hero is immune.

5

A maintenance worker
Was made aware, on a different day,
Of a different shape: Of petals and billows,
A dodge, an opaque ruse,
Expressed by the hunted in their escape
Expressed like the shadow cast by the soul
In flight from hammer and hanging nail
And the death-blow stake. The scream
Formed a blossom, a blot that seemed
One short moment to block out thought,
Just as the body blocks out light,
Leaving only a trace as evidence,
Much less than the weight of existence,
Even lighter than lead in the firing yard
Where the condemned criminal
Bites down hard on the inbound shot,
And the peace of self-assassination
Is stopped and caught
Between unwilling teeth.

6

A motorcycle throttle twists,
The V-Twin engine roars.
It ricochets, burps and wallows
Through urban mist and red brick shadows.
It travels through vast ear canals,
Alleyways and folklore channels
Of the hidden Mnemonic City
Built over ages by refugees,
Seekers, sellers, sidewalk prophets.
And the old municipal library halls
Still echo with lost animal calls
Of the land before they came,
And the shape-note salad of human masses
Rise as a choir from a long, hard past.
The tide of truth becomes a flood,
As workers begin to swim in dread
That the world will end and they'll die alone
Strapped down in their fated beds.

7

A engineer calls out in the early rain
As an elevated-train of celebrants
Crosses the Unreal City,
High, haloed, and without pity
In the butter color of dawning light.
Green El cars pass hard edges
And herald the death of night.
Sharp angles and corners take up the task
To edit the hour like a venery knife
Severing ties binding life to life.
And under the iron tracks of these
Tangled trains of association,
The autos below all have flat tires,
Their identity plates have long expired.
Exhausted by roads run without ends
Corroded by care over many years
Old frames covered in primitive flowers
Watered by immigrant tears.

8

A worker fries her breakfast,
Stares to the opposite building where
Fellow workers stare back.
Between them nothing but TV shows
And grainy, conductive air.
Footsteps click across paving bricks,
The train track sparks and flashes,
An old pipe smoker strikes a match,
And the mannequin god of this rigged clock
Does a mating dance on a music box.
The alarm is rung with a bullwhip crack,
Lifetimes of years pass in a pack.
And the howls of the wolves of industry
Are carried down long dark tubes.
At the end of the hunger, the end of the line
The freighted train of the worried mind,
Meets another looking-glass
Melted by sorrow and falling as tears.

9

There is an old story that seldom gets told
Of an older crime than ours,
And this is how that story goes:
Souls without bodies, children without fear,
Unafraid of repeating floods.
Living on vessels that never find ports,
Dive naked in gold mornings,
In blue afternoons and midnights too,
Down to ancient coral shoals
Retrieving the precious colored buttons
They'll use to shield their eyes
To worship the Blinding God in Regress
As they dance on decks in pagan dress.
Their flexible voices carry their cries
High up the indifferent swallowing skies.
Cistern voices that mimic the curves
Of broken promises, dogma and lies
That twist, collide and swerve.

10

It is a human joyful dirge,
This squealing, squeaking grind of life.
Heard in the bedsprings under the lovers,
Heard in the sine waves of the night,
Heard in the hinges, grates, and gates,
Heard in the wind in the water pipes.
It threatens to surge and topple the masts
Upsetting the pitch of the failsafe craft
With pleas from a future oppressed state
"Save us, Save us!" But we can't.
And this is the crime, surrounding
The doubt, arresting the cancer,
Within the singing, craving heart
Of the workers and artists whose dreams
Had served as matter to start.

11

Beware the meaning in shapes of air:
A scream may be a system of breathing,
A sigh one frequency of resignation,
A sneeze means freedom for distraught demons,
It's said deep breath is a mindful path,
And laughter is mostly a defensive act.
There are no objects, just mutable foam
Gathered at edges of eyes and tongues,
And the dreaded theories of academe,
The tautologies of religion,
Demean themselves before the breath.
For if a scream is a primal release
Machine pressed out of absence,
There may be no rhythm, no volume,
No tone to tune to and no prelude,
Thematic return, no beginning
To make it new.

12

We empty ciphers of desire,
Roaming deserted, hallowed ground,
Are common and know the need is strong
For guidance, so no one's to blame.
See, anyone might wish to believe
There's someone out there to hear us,
An understanding mind out there
Who cares to think about us,
About you or me, they or we.
It's an old scenario to dream on, though,
Everyone mostly hopes it's so,
And no one needs to leave their home,
But if you do and you happen past
A ringing phone in an empty street,
You might just smile and hesitate,
And feel a need to answer it,
Which makes all the crazy accidents
Of the wild world worthwhile.

stage fright

1

He wrote his name in lipstick,
As the genre demands. He took a drink,
A last resort, and set himself to story—
The tale of a man, a cart, a horse,
A boy and a dog, a teenager, fast cars,
And the woman who came between them.
Neither western nor young adult romance—
It had no location, no demographic.

2

On the mirror track, the road heading back,
The same tale runs from death to birth,
From complexity to simple inception.
The split spine recombines, lobes rejoin,
A bullet backs off cracked glass, shards
Fly out from the severed tenor's throat.
An accordion chords old arias of birth,
Trains crash head-on in rubber-band rhythm.

3

Suppressed acts vent themselves in time.
The ecstatic moment of discovery is this:
We've engaged in conflict missions all along.
The symphony expands and contracts
Tune in. Turn on. Drop out. Sing out.
So many voices demand attention,
Suicide might be immoral, if an obvious
Attempt to silence the stage fright.

4

He wrote on the mirror in lipstick—
Colliding both victim and perp in a name
Prefigured in the crashing of narrative trains.
He didn't think about fingerprints,
Didn't foresee any photographs
Didn't plan for damning evidence.
As if the idea was always to be caught
By setting the stage for punishment.

5

He emptied an envelope on the hotel bed—
Snapshots, documents. Then, after reflection
He tore them up with good reason.
Absence could be a door to pass through
Where every past act was erased or changed
By opening ports to alternate paths.
If the future held sanctuary from the past,
Maybe mistakes could be rectified.

6

He wrote an empty name in lipstick.
There was no point to communication.
That religion of naive tongues and signs
Was a doctrine in which he never believed,
Despite obvious props to identity.
It made his position uncertain.
With nowhere to be, he was running,
And those who followed him needed something.

7

The chase crossed fields and housing tracts,
Ghost towns, rail trestles, charred shells
Of hot rods driven recklessly for thrills.
And there were girls as well—
Young women of inhuman beauty.
And cops! Cops and girls went together
In this genre. The girls had hiding places.
The cops had flashlights.

8

Yet even in such troubled memories,
Where he lived both bound and free,
The membrane between fantasy and life
Was more porous than he'd believed.
Women on one side. Police on the other.
Both demanded explanations,
But to justify himself to accusers
Only provoked further anger.

9

He wrote his name in lipstick as bait.
Whatever had gone so desperately wrong
Returned as dubious narrative chains—
Reality coerced by imagination.
But the river flowed both ways—
This ancestral divide of mind was ill-defined,
And the mirror was complicit.
Physical reality meant nothing to it.

10

Dreams are harsh and absolute—
Needing judgment, morality, tact.
One tries to avoid them. But he'd had his
Dreams and couldn't take them back.
You can't take dreams back, the archetypes claimed,
You can't redeem cowardice by nightmare.
There's no rationale for such behavior—
Not for yourself, or others you create.

11

Space needs irritation to fill it.
Phone calls, burglary, bits and bones.
Of personalities played off each other
In a pointless endgame that mimics war
But not wisdom. And there is no evolution
To justify the landscape. Sleep is dangerous,
But so is the smile of a stranger, or a message
Smeared on a hotel mirror like a kiss.

12

One waits in vain for "The End" in quotes.
The hand on a pen, fingers on strings,
Whatever expression was driving this thing,
The protagonist couldn't comprehend.
The plot seemed off. People who'd been dead
Absolved or disposed in earlier episodes
Kept coming back with agendas, issues,
Personal grievances to resolve.

—

13

See, something had happened during sleep.
Though he wasn't sure he'd been sleeping.
To call it sleep would be a joke.
Revenge? Maybe. Diversion? Possibly.
But certainly not sleep. Sleep was refreshing.
So they say. They, Them, The authors,
The Caregivers. Overseers. But wait!
Did they serve him, or he them?

14

Swallow the multiples or die alone:
The river of sensation, the river of emotion,
All effluvium—TV sets, condoms,
Carriages, cars, the dreams of youth—
All flood back from the erotic politic.
In a strange sexuality—foreboding, prophetic,
Yet still "Chapter One"—no time had passed!
Though new life had been born and elapsed.

15

If he could only go back to an origin.
If only he could wake one lovely day
On a small town park bench
On a summer morning, with no evil intent,
Without past or responsibility—
A boundless, anonymous character again,
With both the burden and joy of Free Will
Still unquestioned by him.

16

But you can't take dreams back, this is known,
The membranes are simply too porous.
This man who once craved existence
Had said it to the mirror many times.
He had no identity, no strength to claim one,
And the lipstick smeared on the looking glass
Seemed like a message from a fictional past,
Whose author was sadistic.

17

The actor on stage struggles to evolve—
To reach the heights, one plumbs the depths,
Through hell to heaven, jungle to Eden.
He or she who'd save their life must lose it.
The spiritual battlefield cannot be virtual
Or reduced to surrogate action.
And killers who believe themselves to be
Soldiers of virtue are mistaken.

18

The blade thrust in jest
Is drawn back belted with blood.
The players are shocked, dumbfounded.
Are they victims of their audience?
Is some unknown momentum at play?
Whatever the case, a tragedy occurred
That was not in the script. But really it was!
When read between the lines.

19

What it all boils down to is this:
An individual, once born, must do something,
And every act is the rarest of acts.
Consider the one-in-one-billion
Gene combinations that grant personality,
Physical, mental, direction and drive.
The narrative of a story will fall out.
The protagonist has no real agency.

20

Imagine a car moving toward the future,
And silhouettes of two men seen from the back
As headlights hollow out a road ahead.
Are they scared of what they intend to do,
Of being alone with each other?
Are they frightened to be merely human,
Or by the creeping suspicion they might not be
Human anymore?

21

Somewhere outside town, a train
Pauses at midnight without reason,
Not a station or switching yard, just a stop
On the reversible rubber band plain.
The engine waits, its ditch lights dimmed
While a car pulls into the driveway
Of a quiet suburban home. The car doors close.
Muffled voices carry softly.

22

There's a shotgun in the trunk,
A roll of duct tape and nylon rope.
The nuclear family, no longer asleep,
Hear a noise close by in their quiet street.
A frightened look passes among them.
A shadow crosses the threshold.
The nervous father, out on the porch,
Searching the source, finds only himself.

23

The poison is disguised as milk.
The Child Swallower, the Infant Devourer,
The Infinite One in the loving lap
Of mortal limits considers the trap.
As the Mother intended to poison her Babe,
But the child drinks her dead instead.
Consuming her toxin, the child grows pure
Until virtue destroys the earth.

24

Days earlier, at his hometown Bus Depot,
A man steps into the street,
With only a phone number, duffel and pack.
He stares at the monotone landscape,
Looks for a sign that will never come,
And with hesitant, wandering step,
Into the Garden of Ignorance,
Takes his endless solitary way.

variations on the hunger of angels

1

I hand you, bluntly, a suicide gun.
Be brave, I say, asking your envy to end
My run as benefactor, scapegoat, provocateur,
And in that moment, as an avatar of you,
I feed your ego as I feed your flesh.
We two consummate and we divide
On the issue of who destroys whom.

2

If I call you an angel, the cause is just:
An angel is a second, a specter as guide
To worlds we cannot physically touch.
But if I do touch worlds through you,
If I travel by your light, combined
With my desire, you serve as my bridge
Across realms that split without reason.

3

Existence entertains because it abrades.
The contained in turn contains—
There are heads within our heads,
Eyes inside our eyes. Vision hurts.
And symbols are rendered impotent
By their many diverse frames, as worlds
Collapse only to return again.

4

Do you remember now? You? Me?
How we joined forces in regression.
Back when the blood sea reigned supreme,
Back in the hospital where mating began—
The injection, the dropper, the clear narcotic
Mixed in waters of self regard,
Mistaken as prophylaxis.

5

Angels conjugate the voids, they say,
Feeling a duty to explain things away,
And they do—both for me and for you,
In carbon clocks, arboreal rings,
Molecular metronomes. It seems a lot,
But the goal may be less. For less is more
If regression liberates the future.

6

Male or female, hermaphrodite or parasite—
Atom or the act? The thing in itself,
Or merely the spin? A premonition of more?
Is there beauty before the body is born?
Are angels a project of anxious minds
Seeking to rest in pleasing forms,
Or is beauty a trap, a test by seduction?

7

Child-divinities vie to guide us,
Dressed as transitional beings in silk,
Sackcloth, animal skins, coarse tree bark—
Polysexual Hindu Demons, Fairy Christian Saviors,
The yin-yang tumult of the Acrobat Sophia.
The lie of divinity baits the pilgrim
To hermetic, misanthropic extremes.

8

The serpent/worm was a mouthpiece once
Of a god in which I did not believe.
Though I felt the lowly, the mixed were holy,
And the joining of warring body parts,
Like contradictory thoughts, were signs,
Heralds of the shifting mechanics of mind
What turned wanderers out of Eden.

9

I have many strange confessions to make,
And I don't desire to make them.
I hide them in willful, confused speech.
Thus I defer them and defer to them.
This is how those who live in confinement
React to space, how pariah and exile
Create grace from certain decay.

10

Words can twist aversion to love.
Can compassion be found in fear?
Is the abject a proper product of faith?
Should rhetoric cause unsought events?
Is there that much power in shapes of the air?
Is there so much affect to intent?
Or responsibility to creation?

11

Criminal psychiatrists plague themselves:
"What synapses fired in the brain of the killer,
And what words sparked the act?"
They take tissue from the rectum and tongue,
Cite sensitivity to initial conditions,
The butterfly effect—creation or death?
There's no single agent or cause to suspect.

12

They study the sweat of armpits,
The chemical make-up of kisses and spit.
Analysis makes for a good storyboard.
They look at the problem on microscope slides,
A film-frame progress of the body/mind drive.
Liability begins in saliva and semen.
Guilt by amniotic fluid! Trial by secretion!

13

Things happen in the heat. Psychic forces
Released and read by balkanized minds
Invite persistence in an ignoble cause.
In the end it's always something said
That flowers and spreads to further acts.
One man punches another for a thrill
And the knuckles toll like graveyard bells.

14

Horse flies bite in Mediterranean cathedrals,
Doves flutter before sooted windows,
A decaying whale carcass disrupts summer,
A wolf howls oval cones of horror.
Hurricanes break from a bullet hole—
You can't judge an image by just what it shows,
There's too many ways to read this world.

15

I go to the greenhouse when I want to read
Patterns unspoiled by human needs.
Let comprehension precede consciousness,
Understanding precede the goal to control—
This is the mind of No Mind,
The truth behind the dogma of "Truth,"
The journey begun before there is road.

16

I study close the codes without voice
And pray silence matters in this realm
Of relentless noise and demanding choice,
And to help in my quixotic quest—
I sip black liquor from a leg bone flask,
Take nurture from a Kapala skull cup/bowl,
Purchased at the used parts market of the soul.

17

In the summer of a year lost to inertia,
I met a woman of particular genre,
And I said proudly, "Pain provides our boundaries.
Please outline me against eternity." And she
Replied, "I can't produce the tragedy you need.
I seek my own noose, my own tightrope."
But I wasn't asking for drama, just hope.

18

"Then beware what you request,
Or I'll dress you down in a habit of submission,
And paint you in colors of your conquered spirit."
She added bright feathers and layered on wings,
Multiplied my eyes to muddle her facets.
Friends greet me today with surprise: "You survived!?"
But what does it mean to survive?

19

I never felt so visible, I never felt so capable,
I never felt so laughable, and I wondered
Did she want to bring about my end
By drawing attention to my failings
In this predatory world of false allies
And friends, where passion makes us objects,
And jealousy makes us targets.

20

She and I were as painted birds
Tempting fate in a culture of hunters.
I wondered if this is what psychiatrists meant
By the "Drive to Death" and I wondered
What offspring we could expect,
And how our spawn would direct history
If history would be left to direct.

21

For if we can believe in any thing—
Can we really believe in anything?
And what does belief really mean?
There are so many sides to everything.
Mobs assemble for rights to imitation,
And the masses stage a daily parade
Cheering chaos over certainty.

22

Where the air is course with the grain of time,
Where, at the speed of light, the time
For doubt to flicker and seed
Is the time by which paradise is lost.
Logic grows weak and self-reflection
Seems vain and overwrought compared
To the lethargic pulse of the void.

23

I had little control over my reactions.
Swallowing the sediment, the flotsam
Of the image flood—it didn't go down easy,
But it was never meant that I should be
Comfortable (nor anyone for that matter),
Unease was a goal to strive for,
Along with the promise of something more.

24

A carburetor swallows a fruit fly,
The opera plot spikes in a city siren,
The musical comedy shrinks to an alms plate,
A bead of sweat breaks like an earthquake.
You get off on mutations before you give in.
In the end there's no question that winners don't win,
The first is last and later is always now.

25

The disease feeds off celebrity.
The loop from the mirror is always hungry.
People laugh and ask if I'm insane
To celebrate what devours me?
I reply that I live in a ravenous society
Where gluttony brings cathartic joy,
And psychic wounds are badges of valor.

26

Look at these scars!
Are they not the result of aesthetic disputes?
The tracks on my cheeks may be a trend!
I've seen this culture dissolve in swipes
And sheers of lies and colored lights,
As the human measure of communal life
Takes authority from increased friction.

27

Frequency, duration, spin and vibration,
Line, number, vector: properties exist
In the absence of signified objects.
Inside, outside, imagination, reality:
Every entity speaks with every other entity.
Each thing imitates, perpetuates, itself.
Archetypes cheat death by drift and iteration.

28

All cause is echo, thought is afterthought,
Progression is only illusion.
Reflection derives from a Will to Separate.
Science or faith? Decision or fate?
Creation is always immanent, yet
Creation should be embarrassed to speak,
Fearing a lack of profundity.

29

The rules of engagement are hardly extreme.
Avoid morbidity. Rise above sentiment
And mediocrity. Seek inspiration, not piety,
And if you cry out, be not devout,
But realistic. Transform trauma to inspiration.
Expand and repeat. Add an egg to the soup.
Let the finite thought seed regeneration.

30

Let me tell you an indulgent story:
I watched comrades of the high poetic days
Turn to businessmen, clerks and conmen,
Numbers addicts and information foremen.
I didn't want that technical death, but then
How is this different—this submission
To fantasy the culture suggests.

31

I can think of all rationalizations,
Attack all emotions from multiple sides,
But I can no longer judge what it is that I feel
Or how strong I feel it. Does anybody care?
I imagined I did, or wanted to.
But I didn't at the same time.
I couldn't make up my mind.

32

I was just trying to stay in play with the real—
Ambiguity was my strategy.
I watch what passes for empathy in others—
It does nothing to relieve me.
I see the day go by, I do things,
But it doesn't seem I'm really living.
I get no pleasure from giving or receiving.

34

To find or refine our present incentive,
Stealing a past both real and invented,
It is necessary to punctuate time,
Fill gaps in thoughts with facts, events,
Instinctual acts with proper intention.
Or so the muse countered my plea.
Living by speed, she said, is just reeling,

35

But if we live too fast we diffuse ourselves
In the high shrill whine of granular life.
We chafe and grate and irritate ourselves—
A constant reminder of how small we must be.
Sure, it's nice to kick back,
Cultivate the beauty of a nervous habit.
Compliments and insults are freely exchanged.

36

And the best to offer a hand in this
Must be a clown, a contrary man,
Who does everything against the grain,
A topsy-turvy Lord of Misrule,
A side-eyed Prophet, a Holy Fool.
Who can't impose truth on fiction,
But he can move against blind conviction.

37

In such manner I turned to my consort
To verbalize my conflicted desires.
But she was not as I pretended.
My passivity made unwanted demands.
They broke her, exposed her,
Until the sum of ill-fitting parts
Was smaller than her whole.

38

But you never believed me, did you?
And you're not the one that matters here
Are you? What matters is force of spirit.
If I stopped fixing myself on its promise
I might turn to hate by instinct.
Perhaps I do and I don't know, but if it's so,
To whom do I direct this animus?

39

Too old to learn to talk new ways or prey,
Don't let it get away like I did.
Or maybe you should just let it go.
Open the book. Open the window. Read to create.
The pantheon was never only your own.
At some point words will turn on you.
And you'll search in another mind for a home.

40

Beware that home where self attacks self,
Where spirits face off without theater masks
To compound their emotions.
The dialectic of This vs. That, infinitum,
Is often poetic, but more likely pathetic.
And with that in mind, I rose to the task
Of expecting no conclusion or return.

41

But that was long ago. And long ago too,
Were those who posed as my guardians.
They set up sessions with therapists
And priests concerning my "condition."
They called my visions gratuitous and pagan.
They said I had a problem. But that's all over.
I don't think like that now.

42

I remember only separation and clash,
Between all betweens. But there was no
Continuum from presence to absence,
There was a flash almost violent that ended
In silence. It was nothing, really nothing,
Yes, it was nothing at all brought me
To this threshold of Being but you.

43

I refer here to discord evolution
Of the aggregates whereby the "We" began,
So let us return to constructed beginnings.
You and me—back to pinpoint one,
Back to our parting. Remember
The mirror? Remember the gun?
Remember when we two were one?

44

In a pastoral two children played
Alive with promise, naked, chaste.
I held out a suicide gun and asked:
Destroy me as lover, benefactor, maker,
And in that moment, I will become
As you'll always be to me—a coffin nail,
A wing of wax. But I took that offer back.

45

It makes no sense to create more pain,
For if I lose you and you lose me,
We'll be alone. Ignorant and free.
But we're already outside those walls now,
The danger is too well known now,
And we can't decide if we can, or want to be,
Alone in our knowledge anymore.

after thoughts of a travel-worn satchel

"Coming home at last
At the end of the year,
I wept to find
My old umbilical cord."

scratching after

As spring progresses to fuller costume,
Filling interstitial space
And the ragged art of the barren
Striving branches is further obscured
In broad leaves, succulent flowers,
Seed pods, falling feathers and bird song,
Spring life may be a thing
To celebrate for color and seduction
But I lose those winter friends,
My comrades in anxiety.

For I've always felt an empathy
With those yearning limbs,
Scratching after sustenance
In their multiple, abstract ways.
We all go after light that isn't gained
Without fight and sacrifice
Such as dormant trees express
In the grasping designs I cherish.

If only I could grow my own
Limbs and tributaries, like a Hindu deity,
To end my arms with many implements
Of war or devotion—
Paintbrush, pen, sword or baton.
As it is, I'm covered with blossoms
Of my deeds: facial expressions
Multiplied by age and emotional displays
That cover my essence.

Summer may be the great disguise,
Stage paint meant only to seduce,
Feed and propagate,
But the telling winter always returns,
When, like the dormant trees, I too expose
The yearning bones of the paths
I've taken over many years—
A weather-beaten skeleton
Of visible decisions
Showing what I've become
And where I wanted to go.

the robing

What we breathe repeats in rolls of riddles,
        In echoes of erotic notes, from feathered throats,
        From rain choked waterboard songs
Of visions incoming, relentlessly flushing, tossing,
        Hauled to & from far ports by freighter loads,
        Conflicts, customs, costumes,
Sounds as yet untried by the polyglot tongue,
        Kletzmer clarinets & tubas, klaxon horns,
        Harmonicas of glass, plaintive sweet as oboe grease
And savory as petal tar on painted space
        Where planets spin in histrionic mists,
        Of myriad perfumes & apothecary tonics,
While spears of light & subway trains,
        Run wormholes through the cities of the mind,
        And the skeletal frames of past gestalts,
Of stone & steel & sap-filled scaffolds,
        Hold fertile hearts that pump with passion,
        Histories of hate, religion & race,
And the blood wells, ice flows, locks loose,
        Sewers surge, then flood & plunge
        To cathedral shadows in back alleys,
And sacred pools where paper boats, bodies, barges,
        Rise & fall on tidal urges
        Of high desire & hormones wild,
And the currents of the cloying main stream
        Meet the fractal arrays of chaos,
        Machine made or played in the slow,
Sentient crepuscule of evolution's blink,
        Wherein a greenest bottled light still falls
        Through floral, leafed out canopies,
Twinkles across vast pond skins of deceit & protection,
        And coats in honey, those closet worlds
        Of dreaming children in their secret space,
While the red plains all around them burn,
        With tribal conquest, jealous deities, industrial unrest,
        And dead currency piled & set in flames,
As the hiss of dust & whirl wind carry
        Operatic odors plump with scents
        Of desert & dark jungle, Edens of Evil

Eroding all foundations, geological & civil,
 And the crashing plates of mountains,
 Meet furrows made by train wrecks in the brain,
Listen up! It shouts. A bus goes by a block away,
 We feel it in our hi-wired spines,
 Even rolling in raw rose beds, knowing
Joys & thorns of sorrow, carnival nights of fire flies,
 Kora, bagpipe, xylophone delights, while trombone
 Slides rise to skies in wisdom trees
As notes unfold to minds in flight, bounced about
 By bumpers, back & forth as if struck
 By a drunk driver weaving, or a truck
Careening, no brakes, headlights dead, a comet
 Off course on a light-years-long ride
 Filled with hollow head-talk,
And for all this, we, each one of us,
 With & without guilt, perp-walk,
 And strut our stuff with dubious pride
Across vast landscapes of ancestry,
 As the never virgin, ever virgin world
 Teases each step to arousal, each seed
And what seems to us a limit to our thought balloons,
 Those far reaches of emotion's skin,
 They swell and speak through open pores:
Beware! The urge to simplify the moment is a risk,
 For we will always wear the world
 In all its wonder, all its war,
We are never just our naked selves,
 We are forever clothed in robes,
 Worn tomorrow as worn before.

disappearance of the prophet

Whoever hunts the trophy of the heart
Hunts as well the heart's hunter
And the sorrows just under
The veil of reflected light
Where water flower mouths
Sound warnings from the river beds,
Mud lands, caves and hidden coves.
There's ancestry to be traced
In the blind continuity of species
Preserved in the pressed oil,
Coal and bone of forebears,
A language meant to bind past
And future to the uncouth shapes
Flesh takes over ages.

But what of the wannabe possessors,
Those librarians, poets and killers
Who tug the webs, fishing lines and nets
That serve each species' need
To distinguish enemies
In the formless mess of sensation,
To draw nurture in the liminal
Drain lands that dot and ring
The edges of so many ignorant maps
Before difference destroyed
Their common bonds.

There, in heart-formed corridors
Of forest, swamp, body and mind,
There, on back roads of gravel
And grave dirt leading nowhere special,
Prophets are seen trudging along,
Following the path of this or that cliché.
The eyes of innocents are treasured
By such tramps on futile missions,
Like pretty rocks in a hitchhiker's pocket,
Or lucky dice of human bone
In a gambler's travel satchel.

On a fruitful summer afternoon
As everything repeats itself,
One of this often iterated breed
Takes leave of comfort, revives
Some houseboat or broken skiff
Long swamped in shore reeds
And drains it, patches the scarred,
Watch-eyed birch skin,
Fills it with useless provisions
And reins it to the wanton swans
Of different storylines, pulling
Toward different ends.

As to the moral of the journey—
No cartographer, no student
Of the ravenous continents,
And off-kilter towns, no pilgrim
On the faded, infolded cannibal
Roads of the anxious mind,
Upon reading the scroll
And stalking the moment
To its remote birthplace
With oil lamps and mason-jars
Could quite remember the why of it,

Though many patrons
Of the wayside hostels proclaim to this day
To have known some such hunter,
Some beer hall rogue, drunken bard,
Misbegotten renaissance troubadour
Or bodhisattva bad boy just off the bus,
Backpacking to El Dorado or Valhalla,
Who passed through once,
Seeking a lesser way to the throne
Of the timeless, a way
That couldn't be known
Or played like a stage.

In quest of hearth
He found himself, as foretold,
Hunter and hunted at once.
On the Doorstep of the Temple.
Challenges were laid down.
Some say shots were fired,
Harsh words exchanged,
But one fact remains,
He was never heard from again,
So most conclude he collapsed
Into dust in bliss or humility
On seeing himself as he was.

Yes, he simply disappeared,
Like a would-be prophet should,
From all the stories and myths
That would have caged him
And his wild predictions.
And that may be a problem
With claiming special vision,
But it's also the gift.

the Indifferent witness

Beneath the lotus-petals of any illusory surface
That hides origins from further ambitions,
Forgotten species given to extinction still exist,
Like the crusty, ill-humored Coelacanth
Suspended with its beard of broken hooks,
Due many sad Ahabs come and gone—

Just another stand-in for the indifferent witnesses
Who cannot hear the worming wind
Sing through desiccated cages of has-been
Concepts dotting the bone hunter's plain,
Where paleontologists shed water-color tears
For the futility of their discipline,

So many indifferent witnesses survive,
Who cannot hear the pounding war hooves
Across the battlefields and bombed out streets,
Or breathe the toxins of the turpentine camps,
Or feel the coal dust clotting miner's lungs,
Or hear the circuit-weavers laugh
As they wire death forward in commerce.

So many indifferent witnesses living without passion,
Who cannot know seductive scents
Of once clean bed linens, distressed
And left to air their stains, nor can they imagine
The red muscled machine of tendons, nerves
That glorify this landscape, nor understand
The word threads waving with false promises,

So many indifferent witnesses, so willingly blind
To injustice, brutality, and the dignity of voices,
Varied in their timbre, yet sourced in primordial
Rhythms running unheard on the filaments
Behind many modern lover's eyes—
Strings that tremble with human exultation,
Guilt, humiliation, and childlike surprise.

a demon haunted world

Just up the hill from the old barn,
Well beyond the last failing street light,
The glow from domestic windows
Can't be seen for the spruce fingers
Reaching into the roadside
And the whirling fogs of confusion.
This is the dominion of darkness,
Where the only sounds heard are mixed
Vectors of winds, waving limbs,
And the only movements are moon
Shadows, blown ghost shapes
Capes, cowls and wandering wraiths
Of the old ways: those vague imaginings
Of the myth bred mind.
It's there I crouch in false solitude,
Read the rumors with ancient nerves
Of those who lived long before
The noise of reason and machines.

I erase the explanations
And structures that raised me,
Revisit a world without science,
A haunted realm of beings unbound
By numbers or cause/effect physics,
Where the feral expressions of night
Don't sustain or obey our laws,
Where the didgeridoo deep incantations
Of wind snakes and werewolves
And the ululations of unseen throat singers
Affect my mind with threat and quest,
Determined that I should know
What a sorry small thing I am,
Squatting there, a would-be human,
A failed shaman, with an ear wide-open
To the storm drain of a world,
Too fantastic to tame
But too seductive to fully fear.

the compassion of the inanimate

An old proverb says: Cut yourself
On the edges of physical presence.
Pain and discomfort can ground you,
So treasure this sacred affliction.
It's why we reach for the thorn bush
Despite misgiving. Why we grind our
Teeth to the root despite future hunger.

Jewels, stones, bones and utensils
Collected over years like coins,
Worn and mysterious, eyeglass frames,
Buckets of rusted pocket knives,
Old watches, springs and screws,
Ceramic doorknobs; stuff runs through
Your fingers like a river from paradise.

And I'm here to say the concepts
Of the mind are physical as well,
Born in blood, feces, and electricity.
The currents of wind, water, earth
Pass thought forms through our lives
Like old cloth bound books whose spines
Are separating from their pages,

The library is vast.
Compassion may enlarge you
But what you touch extends you too.
Let such thingness grow existence.
Sensation against even calloused hands
Wires one out in infinite tendrils,
So try to hold on as best you can,
At least until the hard rains come.

adventures in tinnitus

Perhaps I strain to hard to hear it:
The sirens, riots, crowds in rapture,
Where none actually exist,
Even as I run the streets to chase
That life of the city to its lair,
I realize it's in my head.

For instance, up country,
There's that summer I looked
Forward to the cicadas of Brood X
As if it were an upcoming music festival
For which I'd bought a ticket,
Anticipating a night-long merry-go-round
Rhythm section of call and response,
Hoping to sing myself into it.

But when the season arrived
I didn't hear them,
I only thought I heard something,
But it was actually the rushing
Of distant river water
Mixed with the periodic pulse of traffic
Mixed with the stop and go
Tinnitus of my isolated mind.

Down in the valley,
Through the pines and shrubs,
One night I heard the chanting of Satan
Worshippers in the abandoned house
As they praised the lambent moon.
I always knew they might be in town.
This landscape of ruin demands a cult.
Come morning, however, that house was empty.
It was only tinnitus mixed with alcohol
And my desire to make a scene.

Often in the evening,
Laying in bed or reading
In my rocker before the fire,
But also not reading, because the world
Is too close and intimate,
The voices of dead lovers whisper beside me,
Hissing and licking the inside of my head
With judgmental tinnitus tongues.

And of course, there's always
The ringing of a distant
Non-existent phone to prick my fears.
It's an old horror film cliché.
As they say: Get out. Get out.
The call is coming from inside the house.
And, of course, it really is.
It always is.

the handprints of cave children

Animal maps are chemical,
Scents, colors, magnetic fields,
Starlight ways, excremental trails,
But human maps are metaphors,
Tales of borders, land tamed
And how to cross with purpose:
Turn left at the dead white pine
Just north of the gravestone rock,
Angle thirty-degrees off the cairn,
That deer path will lead
Direct to the old miller's field,
Follow the broken stone wall
To the stream ford, 20 paces left
There's a hole in the fence
Through which you can view
The future you seek.

Whose woods these are
I do not know, but if I venture long
The road noise fades, the unbound
Forest sounds signify something
To some creature, tree or weed,
But not me. This gift of unknowing
Spreads in many directions,
But the summons is dangerous bait.
Go ahead, it says, let the green-drive lead,
Climb the scrub and thorn covered hill
And, suddenly, there's no way home,
Though maybe there is an undiscovered
Ocean or canyon beyond the ridge,
A waterfall, chasm or glen
Filled with bestial butterflies.
The accidents of creation can still
Surprise us: Flocks of Aurochs,
Ostriches, Dodos, a racing herd
Of Raptors thought long extinct.

I have no promises to keep
In this unpromising place.
The woods are endless and deep,
Monotonous, deceiving,
Littered with rusted cans,
Beer bottles, fish tins,
Shreds of a torn tent—leftovers
Of those who passed before,
Evidence of a more invasive
Species than beetles or weeds,
And I wonder, as one of them,
Were I to make camp here,
Would I even survive inspection,
Knowing I'm never alone,
That everything alive and not
Views me with suspicion.

And if I were to die here
In some unsung hollow,
Or beside a stagnant lagoon,
Would absent spirits sing to my sleep,
Would their sighs summon more rogue
Explorers, who, like myself,
Come naked, searching answers,
Searching for the handprints
Of cave children, painted in stains
Of ochre and ancient berries,
Small hands reaching tentatively
Forward in time to warn us
Against ourselves.

uptown summer

Spirits wander without goals,

Versifying in gutters, shaping noble myths,
Or itching in poor taste among empty lot weeds

Where the o-mouths hit operatic pitch
And are answered from the lurid recess,

Of this busy little, dense little, crying
Humid surface of an overworked crust,

Sucking flower heads mid summer,
As record heat blows the muscle fibers up,

Every liquid morning, porous evening,
Squeezing the season down receptive cells

Till it all rolls, flows, moving by beneficial
Trade of head-space and caloric degree.

Avalanches of future ecstasy crash, symbols toll,
Drums summon blood and bile by genetic decree.

A cool breeze incites applause,
Baggy skins flap in the dirty dusk of gangways,

And the dripping tongues of the geisha tree fans
Draw a ball-bearing verge,

As they spank quick shadows down long broad halls
Of mazy neighborhood streets

Where human spillage acts
Little dramas out on stoops,

And whispering t-shirt, one-man tribes compete
With screams of cracked cicada tombs,

And the reproductive drive,
That misguided lust of yearning broken things

Under 3rd degree lunar heat,
Make of the city a fool's crown,

Swarming with flies, moth wings, coyote cries.
Hands, thews, wombs wave in the market breeze,

Insects hunger through their fickle forms,
As the drawn-out bang and clamor of rail brakes

And the iron bridge's hinge grates harmonize
With bull doves grunting gruff on window sills

In this world the senses paint so plain,
Even if our words corrupt.

the fall

I fell in a hole once
And just kept falling
Figuring to hit the hard place
That would be my end.
But the bottom never showed,
I continued going down,
Flailing like a helpless ill-fated
Clown looking up in horror
As the rim of the world disappeared
Like an iris closing out the light.
Eventually I realized
The fall would never end,
It was just the way things were,
A metaphor for the drop away
From all things certain or solid:
The fall from innocence,
The fall of atoms in the void,
The fall from the face of one's beloved.
But once I gave up the thought
Of hitting any bottom,
Once I gave up hope,
I was free to enjoy the journey.
The speed of passing varied scenes
Became passionate music.
My gesticulations turned to dance moves,
Watusi, jig, twist and hustle,
For the past had disappeared
And the future was nothing at all.
I'd abandoned expectations
For the joy of, if not freedom,
At least some profound lack
Of containment
By which I could feel alive
For the first time.

Carl Watson is a poet and novelist, born in Northwest Indiana, living in New York City and the Catskill mountains while hiding out in various other undisclosed locations.